Little Fred
Riding Hood

Michael Cox Liz Million

To Jo and Tom

M.C.

For my wonderfully fantastic mum and dad

love from leeby

L.M.

EGMONT

We bring stories to life

First published in Great Britain 1995 as part of *The Independent Scholastic Story
of the Year 3* by Scholastic Ltd
This edition published 2006 by Egmont UK Ltd
239 Kensington High Street, London W8 6SA
Text copyright © Michael Cox 2006
Illustrations copyright © Liz Million 2006
The author and illustrator have asserted their moral rights
ISBN 978 1 4052 1917 4
ISBN 1 4052 1917 3
10 9 8 7 6 5 4 3 2 1
A CIP catalogue record for this title is available from the British Library.
Printed in Singapore

contents

Red Bananas

4

A Trip to Wolfworth's

Wilf Wolf put down his copy of *Little Red Riding Hood* and sighed a big sigh. He gazed at the picture of the Big Bad Wolf on the front cover and said, 'Oh I do wish I could be just like you, Big Bad.'

Big Bad was Wilf Wolf's hero and *Little Red Riding Hood* was his favourite story. He'd just finished reading it for the twenty-third time and he'd enjoyed it more than ever, even though the last two pages were missing.

Whenever he asked his mum where those
two pages were, she always said,
mysteriously, 'There are certain things it's
best for a young wolf not to know
about, my boy!'

Wilf often used to wonder
what happened after the

What happens next, Mum?

bit where Big Bad is in the gran's clothes waiting for Little Red to arrive. What he did know, though, was that he'd love to have an adventure like the one in his favourite book. If only he could bump into a Little Red Riding Hood who just happened to be on her way to her sweet old granny's with a basket full of scrumptious goodies! But he'd never even seen a Red Riding Hood, never mind tasted one.

As Wilf sat daydreaming
about Riding Hoods, his
mum came into his room.
'Wilf, just pop down to
Wolfworth's for me and get
a dozen tins of Happy
Wolf,' she said.

'It's a full moon tonight and I'm inviting
the pack round for a whine and howl party.'

'All right, Mum,' said Wilf. 'I'll get some
Cub Cakes as well.'

On the way back from the shops, Wilf went a new way home. As he turned the corner into a strange street he saw something that made his paws twitch with excitement.

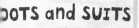OTS and SUITS   WOLFWORTH'S   KITES and

In the front garden of a
house, a small boy thing
was waving to a sweet
old granny thing
and the
small
boy thing
was wearing a . . .
RED HOOD!

11

Wilf wanted to howl with joy, but he
didn't – he clapped a paw over his snout
and quickly hid behind a bush to
watch the scene.

Bye bye, my little angel!

'Bye-bye, Granny,' said the boy thing.
'Bye-bye, Little Fred,' said the granny thing.
Wilf could hardly believe his eyes and ears.

'If I'm not dreaming, this really is my lucky day,' Wilf said to himself, as he watched the granny thing totter off down the road. She was exactly like the granny in the pictures in his book. She had wispy white hair, little round glasses, a walking stick, a bonnet and a shawl. She was perfect!

As soon as she was out of sight, Wilf nipped out from behind the bush and strolled over to the little boy, who was pedalling his bicycle round and round.

In his friendliest voice he said, 'Hello, small boy thing!'

'Hello, fungus face!' said the boy.

'What a rude child!' thought Wilf, feeling a terrible urge to eat the boy on the spot – but that wasn't in the story, so he didn't.

Instead he gave him a sickly smile and said, 'And what's your name, little chap?'

Hello, small boy thing!

I'm Little Fred riding good.

'My name's Fred Hood,' said the boy. 'Cor!
You aren't half hairy! Haven't you heard of
shaving? Hey, furry features, watch me ride
my bike. I'm riding good, aren't I? I'm Little
Fred, riding good, I am!'

Wilf couldn't believe his luck! The boy had
said it himself. He was Little Fred Riding
Hood!

'Er . . . who was that little old lady you
were just talking to, Little Fred?' asked Wilf,
trying to control his excitement.

'Oh, that was my dear old granny, whose cottage I often visit carrying a basket full of scrumptious goodies,' said the little boy. 'My old granny is ever so sweet.'

'I bet she is!' said Wilf, drooling and licking his lips hungrily. By now he was quivering all over with excitement.

'Anyway, what's it got to do with you, you old slobber chops?' said Little Fred. 'And why are you shaking – are you cold?'

'Yes that's it,' said Wilf. 'I'm c-cold. I've got to go now. Bye-bye, Little Fred Riding Hood!'

'Oh goodness gracious me!' Wilf thought as
he rushed home to make his plans. 'I'm
finally going to gobble a granny. I'm so
excited, I can hardly wait!'

See you then,
fungus face!

Weirdy Whiskers!

The next morning Wilf got up really early and in no time at all he was on his way to Little Fred's house, singing happily to himself as he went,

'I'm Wilfy the Wolf, I am!
I'm off to gobble Fred's gran.
When I have ate her, I'll feel a lot better.
She'll taste just like
pickles and ham!'

When he arrived at the house he hid
behind the bush and waited. After about ten
minutes, out came Little Fred. He was
carrying . . . a BASKET!

'Wow!' thought Wilf. 'IT'S EXACTLY
LIKE IN THE STORY!'

As calmly as he could, and whistling casually (a wolf whistle, of course), he wandered past Little Fred's front gate. Then, pretending to be surprised to see him, he said, 'Well I never! Little Fred Riding Hood. What a surprise! Fancy bumping into you just here!'

'Don't be stupid, snotty snout! I live here!' said Little Fred. 'Where else would you expect to bump into me? You do talk a load of rubbish, you do!'

Wilf really did want to eat this cheeky child straight away, but that wasn't in the story, so he just said, 'And where might you be going this fine spring morning?'

You gibbering gerbil!

'What do you mean? It's September and it's raining!' said Little Fred.

'It was spring in the book,' said Wilf, looking a bit disappointed.

'What are you talking about, weirdy whiskers?' said Little Fred.

'Oh, nothing, nothing!' said Wilf. 'Which way are you walking? Perhaps we're going the same way and I could walk with you a while?'

'I'm going on the path through the woods to my granny's cottage. It's number 5, Honey Pot Lane,' said Little Fred.

'Oh, that's nowhere near where I'm going. I'm off to visit my aunt in Wolverhampton and I'm three weeks late, so I must dash. Bye-bye, Little Fred!' said Wilf, and he raced off into the woods to make sure he reached the granny's cottage before Little Fred did.

Aha!

I'm coming to get you!

As he ran through the woods, Wilf kept repeating to himself, 'Number 5, Honeypot Lane, number 5, Honeypot Lane.' At last he reached the cottage. It was exactly like the one in the book! It had pink roses around the front door, little windows with flowery curtains and a cat fast asleep on the garden wall.

Tee hee!

Now all Wilf had to
do was knock on the
door and pretend
to be Little Fred
Riding Hood.

He tiptoed up the
path and knocked very
gently on
the cottage door.

'Who is it?' asked
a voice.

'It's me, Little
Fred, your loving
grandson,' said Wilf, in
his squeakiest voice. 'I've
brought a basket of goodies for your tea.'

'Just a minute,' said the voice. 'I'll open the
door.'

Wilf thought, 'This is it! The minute Fred's

granny opens that door I'll leap on her and gobble her up. It's just like the story, except I'm going to be the hero this time. Right, here she comes. Five, four, three, two, one . . .'

There was a rattle as someone fiddled with the latch, then the door creaked slowly open.

'I'm coming to get you!' howled Wilf, as he rushed forward.

In the next instant, Wilf got the shock of his life.

Rather than pouncing on a sweet old granny and gobbling her up before she'd had time to put down her knitting, Wilf found himself staring up at the most enormous old lady he'd ever seen!

She must have been at least six foot tall and her gigantic shoulders filled the doorway of the cottage. She was wearing a purple tracksuit and bright yellow jogging shoes and she was holding one of those weights that body builders use to make their muscles really big. She casually tossed it from one hand to the other as though it were as light as a feather!

GULP!

Wilf was flabbergasted!

'She's definitely not in the book,' he thought. 'Something has gone seriously wrong with my plan! I think I'll just nip off home and re-read this bit.'

But, before he could run away, the giant woman reached down and put one of her massive hands on Wilf's trembling shoulder.

'And what might you be wanting, young fellow?' she asked, in a voice that made Wilf's legs turn to jelly.

'I'm terribly sorry,' squeaked Wilf. 'I seem to have knocked on the wrong door. I was looking for a sweet old lady.'

'But I am a sweet old lady,' replied the woman, twirling the ten kilo weight in her hand and peering suspiciously at Wilf. 'You aren't . . . by any chance, a wolf . . . are you?' she said. 'You do look ever so much like a wolf, you know.'

She peered even closer at Wilf, then gasped, 'Oh, my goodness gracious me, you are a wolf!

Grrr!

'Oh dear, I hope you aren't planning to do something horrible like gobbling up a poor, defenceless old lady!'

She tightened her grip on Wilf's shoulder and lifted him a couple of centimetres off the ground.

'No, no, I'm not a wolf, I promise I'm not,' protested Wilf as he watched his feet leave the ground and dangle in mid-air. 'I'm just a very hairy little boy who likes to go around helping old ladies. No, I'm definitely not a wolf!'

'Oh, yes you are!' yelled a voice from behind him. 'And if you're a hairy little boy, then I'm a giant panda! Who are you trying to fool, fungus face?'

Wilf looked over his shoulder. Little Fred was coming up the garden path.

'You couldn't be anything else with a mush like yours, ferret features,' laughed Little Fred.

Well I never! It's the giant gerbil!

'And what are you doing with my gran?'

Wilf was baffled. 'This can't be your gran!' he said. 'Your gran's small and has got white hair and a walking stick!'

'That's my other gran, budgie brain!' cried Little Fred. 'I visit that gran on Thursdays and this gran on Saturdays.'

Wilf was upset. 'Why didn't you tell me you had two grans?' he asked.

'You never asked me. Anyway, what are you doing at my gran's?'

Before Wilf had time to answer, Little Fred said, 'Hey, you weren't thinking of doing anything naughty, like gobbling up my gran, were you? Come to think of it, I bet you were. You hairy rascal!'

He turned to his gran and said, 'I bet he was, Gran. Just look at him. You can tell he was! Just look at his face!'

Little Fred's Saturday gran turned to look at Wilf's face, but it wasn't there – and nor was the rest of Wilf.

He was galloping down the garden path as fast as his legs would carry him.

'After him, Gran!' yelled little Fred. 'We'll marmalise him, just like the woodcutter does to the Big Bad Wolf in the Little Red Riding Hood story!'

When Wilf heard these words he realised just why his mum would never tell him about the two missing pages in his favourite story, and he began to run about a hundred times faster!

Let's marmalise him!

Don't Marmalise Me!

After he'd raced through the woods for absolutely ages Wilf noticed that the awful little boy and his enormous gran had stopped chasing him, so he sat down at the side of the path for a rest. As he did, he spotted a familiar tiny figure tottering towards him. It was Little Fred's Thursday gran. When she reached Wilf, she put her little wrinkled hand on his shoulder and began to speak.

'Excuse me, young man. I've just dropped my spec–'

But Wilf was taking no chances. He had had enough of grannies for one day.

'No, no! Please don't marmalise me!' he begged the frail old lady. 'I'll be a good boy from now on. I'll never terrorise a granny again. I promise.'

And with that, he ran off yelping, 'I want my mummy!'

Mercy! Mercy!

'What a strange little boy,' said the old lady to herself. 'And so hairy for one so young. There was no need for him to rush off like that. I was only going to ask him to help me look for my spectacles. I hear there are wolves in these woods.'

What a strange boy.

A New Hero!

Wilf eventually reached home, looking rather the worse for wear after his chase through the woods. But at least he was still in one piece! Wilf decided that from now on he was most definitely not going to take any notice of silly stories about the adventures of other wolves. Especially ones involving children and their grannies!

Phew!

When Wilf stepped into the kitchen, his mum gave him a big hug then made him a cup of cocoa. As he sat by the fire with his cocoa and a Cub Cake she said, 'Well, what have you been up to? You look as though you've been dragged through a hedge backwards.'

I'm starving!

'There are certain things it's best for a mum wolf not to know about,' said Wilf, very mysteriously, and went upstairs, leaving his mum feeling a bit bewildered.

Later that evening, after finding Wilf's copy of *Little Red Riding Hood* in the rubbish bin, she went into his room and found him sitting up in bed, reading and looking a lot better.

'You look a bit happier, son,' she said.

'Oh, I am, Mum, I am!' said Wilf. 'I feel loads better. And what's more, I've found this absolutely brilliant new book.

'I think it's going to be my favourite ever.
It's got this amazingly clever wolf in it.'

'That sounds nice, Wilf. What's it called?' asked his mum.

'It's called *The Three Little Pigs*,' said Wilf.